Mitzi
and the Big Bad Nosy Wolf:
A Digital Citizenship Story

by **Teresa Bateman**

illustrated by **Jannie Ho**

HOLIDAY HOUSE • NEW YORK

Mitzi was a fluffy lamb who loved to dance in the meadow near her home.

"Now, Mitzi," her mother told her, "always take a friend with you."

"And Mitzi," her father reminded her, "don't talk to strangers."

There were all sorts of other rules, too, but Mitzi hardly paid attention. She was too busy dancing.

One morning, Mitzi felt the itch in her hooves, and she just knew she had to dance.

But one friend was programming her robot.

And another friend was building a rocket ship. Drat—they were all busy!

So she hurried to the meadow all alone.

9

Mitzi did the tango, the rumba, and the funky
chicken, but still she wanted to dance some more.

While Mitzi was dancing, a stranger wearing a long fur coat slid into the meadow. His nose was long and sharp, but not as sharp as his teeth.

When Mitzi caught sight of the stranger, she remembered her parents' rules, but by then it was too late to obey some of them. She could only hope the rest would come in handy.

"Hello," said the stranger, smoothly. "Don't you look delici . . . er, I mean delightful, dancing here in the meadow. Might I ask your name?"

"Oh no, no, no," Mitzi said. "I don't tell that to strangers. **That's PRIVATE!**"

"Now, now," the stranger soothed. "Your name isn't private. Think of all the people who know it—your family, your friends, your teachers. It hardly seems a secret. Look, I'll tell you *my* name, and then I won't be a stranger at all. My name is Wol . . . er . . . Rolf."

"Wolerolf?" Mitzi asked.

"Just Rolf," the stranger corrected. "It's French and means 'kind and trustworthy friend.'"

Mitzi frowned. She rather thought the name Rolf was German and meant 'noble wolf,' but it probably wasn't a good idea to argue with him.

She needed to figure out how to get away, but he was surely much faster than she was.

"Would you like to dance?" she asked Rolf.

"Why, certainly," Rolf replied. "Come into my arms, my little lamb chop, and we will dance off into the sunset together."

Mitzi smiled. "Certainly, Rolf, but first let me see you do the Charleston."

He picked up his paws and soon they were dancing, side by side. As they danced Rolf panted, "You are amazing. Let me take your picture to put in my recipe boo . . . er, scrapbook."

"Oh no, no, no," Mitzi said. "Nobody takes my picture without my permission. **That's PRIVATE!**"

Rolf was turning red as they shifted to the cancan.

"Perhaps you cancan just give me your phone number or email address so I cancan contact you?" he gasped. "I have some friends in show business who would be quite interested in a tasty . . . er, talented lamb such as yourself."

"Oh no, no, no," Mitzi said. "**That's PRIVATE!**"

The high kicks were a bit much for Rolf. He was relieved when they switched to the twist . . . for a time.

"Please give me your address so I can send you a card for teaching me these amazing dances," Rolf wheezed. "My mother always said to send a thank-you card."

"Your mother is correct," said Mitzi. "But so is mine, and she would say 'Oh no, no, no! That's PRIVATE!'"

"And where might I meet this mother of yours?" puffed Rolf.
    "That's PRIVATE!" Mitzi said.

"Or your father?"
    "That's PRIVATE!"

"Perhaps you could tell me what school you attend?"
"PRIVATE!"

"Or your birthday?"
"PRIVATE!"

By then they had moved through the hora and the Boot Scootin' Boogie.

Rolf was dragging. Even his fur felt tired. He knew he had toyed with Mitzi too long. It was time to act.

Quickly he shouted, "Leap into my arms for a grand finale!"

He held his paws high, ready to catch her, with no intention of ever letting her go.

Mitzi smiled and ran toward him. "Only if you leap, too," she shouted.

He gave a feeble bounce, but it was enough. Mitzi slid right through his legs with pointed toes and perfect form.

"Well, toodle-oo!" Mitzi called out as she skipped away home.

Rolf took two wavering steps after her before he fell face-first in the meadow grass. His nose landed on a daisy. It did not help cushion the fall.

Rolf said something he shouldn't have, but I can't tell you what it was.

It's PRIVATE!

Mitzi's Rules for Digital Citizenship

Being safe is important both in the real world and the digital one. The internet connects millions of computers all over the world—and the millions of people who use them. Just like you follow the rules to be a good citizen in your community, you need to follow the rules to be a good citizen in the digital world. That's called digital citizenship.

It is important to remember that things you do online are not private. Just like when you walk on a beach and leave footprints behind, when you are on the internet you leave behind digital footprints—records of where you have been and what you have done. But unlike a beach, these records don't get washed away with the tide. They can stay there forever. That's why it is so important to be careful.

Here are some smart rules to follow when using the internet:

1. Always ask for your caregivers' permission before using electronic devices.

2. Keep personal information private. This includes your name, age, home address, phone number, email address, photograph, school, and anything else that you wouldn't tell a stranger.

3. Keep the personal information of others private. Don't share information about your classmates, friends, or family without their permission. This includes photographs!

4. Follow website rules, including age-usage requirements.

5. Never copy anything off the internet and present it as your own work. Remember to give credit, cite your sources, and never use copyrighted material without permission.

6. Never use any electronic device to cause harm to another person by harassing, intimidating, or just plain being rude to them. A pattern of this behavior is called cyberbullying. Bullying is never appropriate, whether you're in the classroom, on the playground, or at home on a device.

7. And finally, the greatest, grandest, most glorious rule of all is the "Grandma Rule." Never access or post anything on the internet that you wouldn't want your grandma or even your teacher to see.

   Would you use inappropriate language or show inappropriate pictures to your grandma or your teacher?

   No?

   Then don't post them on the internet!

   Would you say something mean about another person in front of your grandma or your teacher?

   No?

   Then don't post it on the internet!

   Remember, the things you post on the internet STAY on the internet. Never post personal information that you don't want the whole world to see forever, and always tell a trusted adult if something doesn't feel right when you're using the internet.

Glossary

Copyright: the legal right to reproduce, sell, or publish a work, such as a book or a painting

Credit: to recognize or name the person(s) behind an idea or work

Cyberbullying: harassing, intimidating, or being rude to others while using the internet

Digital citizenship: the responsible and safe use of technology and the internet

Digital footprint: a record of everything you do on the internet, including posts, messages, and websites visited

Internet: a worldwide network that connects computers and other devices, like smartphones

Personal information: facts that can identify you, such as your name, age, home address, phone number, email address, photograph, and school

Private: information and places that are for a single person or a small, trusted group

Public: information and places that are open to everyone

Mitzi's Memory Game

1. With the help of an adult, split a stack of eighteen index cards into two equal piles of nine.

2. Write one of the words or phrases below on each of the first nine cards. You can even draw a picture for each!

- **Name**
- **Birthday**
- **Age**
- **Home address**
- **Phone number**
- **Email address**
- **School**
- **Photograph**
- **Where your parents work**

3. Repeat for the other nine cards. You now should have two matched sets.

4. Shuffle the cards so they're all mixed up.

5. Put the cards word side down on a table.

6. Pick two cards and turn them over. If they don't match, turn them back over and try again.

7. Every time you find a match say, "We don't share that information because . . . that's PRIVATE!" Remove the matched sets from the game. Keep going until all the matches have been found.

For Brooklyn, Thomas, Lily,
Henry, and Eli. Some things
are private, so beware.

Sometimes it's better
NOT to share. —T. B.

For Gutsy. —J. H.

Copyright © 2022 by Teresa Bateman
Illustrations copyright © 2022 by Jannie Ho
All Rights Reserved
HOLIDAY HOUSE is registered in the U.S. Patent and Trademark Office.
Printed and bound in September 2021 at C&C Offset, Shenzhen, China..
The artwork was created digitally.
www.holidayhouse.com
First Edition
1 3 5 7 9 10 8 6 4 2

Library of Congress Cataloging-in-Publication Data

Names: Bateman, Teresa, author. | Ho, Jannie, illustrator.
Title: Mitzi and the big bad nosy wolf / by Teresa Bateman ; illustrated byJannie Ho.
Description: First edition. | New York : Holiday House, [2022] | Audience:Ages 4-8. | Audience: Grades K-1.
Summary: Mitzi the lamb outsmarts a nosy wolf, who keeps asking Mitzi personal questions about herself, by
challenging him to a dance-off. Discusses the concept of digital citizenship and provides rules and tips for the
responsible and safe use of technology and the Internet.
Identifiers: LCCN 2021002614 | ISBN 9780823445172 (hardcover)
Subjects: CYAC: Internet—Safety measures—Fiction. | Safety—Fiction. | Privacy, Right of—Fiction. | Strangers—Fiction.
Classification: LCC PZ7.B294435 Mi 2022 | DDC [E]—dc23
LC record available at https://lccn.loc.gov/2021002614

ISBN: 978-0-8234-4517-2 (hardcover)